WATER RATS

BY SIMON OCORRA

© SIMON OCORRA 1ST NOVEMBER 2019

C A S T

Anthonius, Christina's husband

Peter, Anthonius' colleague at the Customs Office.

Myrtle, Christina's Sister

Christina - A woman who lived through the Nazi Occupation of the Netherlands.

Sister Caritas - A young woman soon to be a nun, a contemporary of Christina's. Known to Christina for many years.

Gerrit, Resistance worker

Two Jews and their son

Nazi, an officer who approached Anthonius to have him deliver goods for the Nazis and do other jobs

Another Sister of Christina

Christina's daughter

NSB person trying to jump queue in bakery

Nazi who put NSB person in her place.

Act 1 Scene 1 - Anthonius and Peter a fellow customs officer, in a room in Lobith with confiscated opium which they are beginning to smoke. Discuss what is coming with Nazism 1923 (Jazz music playing on a wind-up gramophone in a small room with two day beds)

Anthonius: This music is the best; it's like it's nothing I have heard before. (*laying back on the day bed*) *The Americans certainly know how to express themselves.*

Peter: I agree (*already laying back on the other day bed*) but not so well as the Chinese HA! HA!

Anthonius: You have a point there. We did well today. The boss will be happy with us.

Peter: Not if he ever realises we have kept some opium back for ourselves. But it's a good idea to try the very thing we are stopping the smuggling of.

Anthonius: I am not sure. Have you read the papers talking of the Chinese people being enslaved by the stuff?

Peter: Come! Join me - let's just try it. Here I'll go first (*preparing to smoke opium*). How bad can it be and more to the point how good can it be? After seeing what I saw in the war believe me I need some distraction.

Anthonius: You're Belgian though. You experienced the war. I didn't, although I have seen what it did to people on all sides.

Peter: It was horrifying. It made us all feel like 'what is the point now' without some fun. Which is why I love music and drink (*raising a bottle of booze*) and anything else which helps me forget. Why should the government get all this stuff? They won't miss a small portion of it. In fact, I doctored the invoice to allow for it. HA!

Anthonius: But is it right?

Peter: There is no right and wrong anymore man. All that shit has gone. They both come from religion and where was God in that conflict?

Anthonius: Religion and God are two different things, or can be. Even if you just choose a personal God unattached to religion then you still must have felt betrayed in those trenches seeing men and animals blown to bits.

Peter: It was horrible, beyond words really. I can never shake those images from my mind and my eyes. I saw a man's head blown off; you don't recover from that.

Anthonius: Your eyes? That is impossible surely.

Peter: Believe me it isn't. The horror of those sights is burned on my cornea because my mind and emotions could not comprehend them.

Anthonius: I understand now.

Peter: Do you? I wish I did. When I drink or smoke the pain disappears for a short while. But it is always there when I come around. Like a conniving ghost. You can never sleep but with one eye open.

Anthonius: We have our families though, our friends. They must help surely.

Peter: Many of them are feeling the same as we do even the non-soldiers. The women are bemused and frightened because we came back changed.

Anthonius: I am planning to find myself a woman who is unafraid. Unabashed and courageous.

Peter: I wish you luck with that. I choose a woman who takes me away from reality. *(pointing to the hookah and the opium waiting on the table which sparest their day beds).*

Anthonius: She will be fickle my friend. She will eat you up.

Peter: Then I am ready to be consumed. She can take me anywhere she likes. *(reaching for some opium and a small Delft opium pipe)* Come my friend say hello to her. Will you take some with me.

Anthonius: In your mood should you really be inflicting that substance on yourself?

Peter: Well if you are so damn cheery why not try it just for fun. *(filling and lighting his pipe and handing it to his friend)* Come on be brave. Your lot didn't fight in the war - at least you can show some damn bravery now. *(he takes the pipe back and takes a huge draw on it and falls back on his bed his hand with the pipe extending to his friend)*

Anthonus: *(taking the pipe and drawing on it delicately)* Alright, I'll have a go. *(Peter takes back the pipe and draws again on it)*

Peter: There you a…….. *(falling back as the drug slowly takes effect)*

Anthonius: Peter, are you alright? *(getting up and shaking his friend who is in another world now)* Damn, that's not what I want, I need my wits about me if I am going to make a success of my life.

Peter: The Weimar Republic in Germany is a good thing my friend. A kind of liberalism is so important after the horrors of the war, (*slurring*) I know it didn't touch us directly but there is a collective consciousness about such savagery taking place so close to your borders. Now we must relax and have fun and explore who we are or at least what is next.

Anthonius: What is next then? Does this drug give you answers? I somehow doubt it. In fact, from what I hear it takes away the questions. The Chinese have it solved, keep the masses in a drug haze in order to control them. They think they are in control but really …..

Peter: What is control though? It has a different perspective for us all.

Anthonius: Oh please. Really? I see now that I am in the wrong business.

Peter: So you want to be in charge or control of the means of destruction?

Anthonius: No I mean I need a new profession. And I need a good woman, a strong woman, a feisty one, one unafraid to live life to the full, willing to give me lots of kids and to grow old with me. I won't find that woman here in this shit hole. There is an opportunity for me in Vreeswijk There's a small bicycle shop available, according to a cousin of mine.

Peter: Where is that? Sounds like a dump. What is wrong with Utrecht?

Anthonius: Best to start small and grow from there. Who knows there may be all sorts of opportunities there?

Peter: You'll always find a way and you don't need to be here by the water to be a water rat. You will always go with the flow as you always have. Seeking new channels and byways.

Act 1 Scene 2 - Meeting Christina a bakery owner at a dance in Vreeswijk. Anthony's cousin owns a bicycle shop but craves a proper garage premises. 1929. Christina's sister is becoming a nun as is her friend Caritas. They are both at the dance before joining the convent.

Christina: This is quite a gathering.

Myrtle: You know what Papa said. We must behave with decorum and mustn't be late home.

Christina: It is only 7.30, We are hardly burning a candle at both ends.

Caritas: You have to be up at 4am. To work and to have the bakery well stocked.

Christina: Unlike you, who gets up at the same time but just to get on your knees and pray.

Myrtle: Don't mock Caritas, Sister.

Christina: You are as bad. Don't try to lecture me. You're just worried the bakery will fail and your damned religious dowry will be used up

Myrtle: I have to have it to get into the convent, you know that.

Christina: What would Mother Abbess say if she could see you now.

Myrtle: It is only one night and our last one at that.

Christina: Sin is still possible in one night (*catching sight of Anthonius and smiling*)

Myrtle: Sister be careful. You know what father says about men.

Christina: And he is one, so let us take his words with a pinch of salt shall we.

Caritas: Wickedness! You should respect your father and trust his words.

Christina: Oh shut up. What do you know of the world? You are cosseted and spoiled. Until you allow yourself to live, then you can't comment.

Myrtle: You are rude Christina. Caritas is an earnest follower and believer.

Christina: I know but you, you are not, you have much going for you, why choose this limiting life? Please do not go. I shall miss you. Everyone else too.

Myrtle: I must follow my own path. I would not dream of stopping you doing what you wish in your life.

Christina: I suppose you are right and I must swallow it and be happy for you.

Myrtle: Yes, do be. Please.

Caritas: That is better, we can only ever live our own lives, not through the thoughts and hearts of others.

Anthonius: What are you girls speaking so earnestly of?

Myrtle: Oh please go away.

Christina: Wait! Remember don't speak for others!

Anthonius: Hello. I am Anthonius. Who are you? What is your name?

Myrtle and Caritas: Don't tell him. You have no idea who he is.

Anthonius: Ladies please, give me a chance. I own a bicycle shop and am doing well. I hope to have a van soon. Things are really taking off for me.

Christina: Sure of yourself aren't you? Girls please mind your own business. Hello. I am Christina. I own a bakery.

Myrtle: It's Papa's actually, she just runs it.

Christina: So it's mine if I run it.

Anthonius: I like your spirit. Care to dance?

Myrtle: Oh no Sister. What would Papa say?

Christina: This is a dance and Papa agreed we could go. So I am determined to dance and not alone. Of course I will dance with you. *(reaching out for Anthonius)*

Caritas: Harlot! does she know no shame?

Myrtle: Don't be like that, she is a good person.

Caritas: She is only as good as her reputation, which has slumped this evening.

Myrtle: Please Caritas, what about Christian charity?

Caritas: For those deserving. The rest can go where they belong *(pointing down to the ground and beyond)* He is a true water rat - look at him, smooth as they come with an answer for everything. Rats may be adaptable on both water and land, but they are still vermin and to be kept at a distance. Your sister has lost all sense of proportion.

Myrtle: Please do not even suggest that. She deserves some fun; she works very hard providing for us all.

Caritas: She takes the profits more like. She is a wrong 'un and it's where she is headed believe me.

Myrtle: Where?

Caritas: Purgatory of course. You are stupid!

Myrtle: *(looking miserable but rousing herself after a second or two)* Oh yes of course. I must re-double my efforts with her, I hope she does not lose her head to that dashing young man. She is headstrong and wild at times but means well.

Caritas: He is like all men - demons one and all. She may mean well too but for goodness sake she will drag your family down to the gutter at this rate.

Myrtle: Not the priests though. Surely not them. They are beyond reproach.

Caritas: No of course not them, they are saints. We are empowered or we will be soon at least with saving souls by whatever means we have at our disposal.

Myrtle: I think my sister needs saving. It has to be possible. She has had too much freedom.

Caritas: If she is not beyond assistance already. You are like chalk and cheese truly.

Myrtle: Isn't that blasphemy? I thought everyone could be saved.

Caritas: That is the official line but let's be honest (*staring at Christina dancing*) There have to be exceptions. It will be our job to discern the depravity of such people and act accordingly.

Myrtle: But do we have that right? I mean Jesus didn't judge, did he?

Caritas: God gives us that right. We are chosen by him to join the discrete group of his followers to have a care for the souls of the sheep. Jesus his son is an idealist, a little liberal at times. Although one has to show him respect as he is God's son. (*Christina and Anthonius return red faced and out of breath*)

Christina: What are you two deep in conversation about? Catechism I bet.

Anthonius: Ladies can I get you a drink?

Caritas: No thank you. We have our own already. We can pay our way thank you.

Christina: What is that, lemonade? I will have a wine please.

Anthonius: Don't go away (*looking intently into Christina's eyes*) I will be back.

Christina: Don't worry I won't (*smiling*)

Caritas: What do you think you are playing at?

Christina: Who do you think you are?

Myrtle: Please. Let's not row.

Christina: Wake up who do you think she thinks she is?

Caritas: I know who I am.

Christina: Do you?

Myrtle: Please Christina do not upset Caritas.

Christina: It is not me. She is upsetting herself. Why are you defending her? You are brainwashed. You are losing all sense of reason and enjoyment.

Myrtle: I am happy.

Christina: Are you? Would God want you to be so miserable.

Myrtle: I told you I am happy, now leave me alone. You need to look at your behaviour. Please don't bring shame on our family. You don't have to become a nun like us but you can moderate your behaviour surely.

Christina: You talk of shame…….

Myrtle: *(looking ashamed)* Come on Caritas this place is not for us. We have seen wickedness for what it is, a wanton indolence and moral depravity.

Christina: Go on then go to your ivory tower, much happiness it may bring you both. *(raising her eye- brows)*

Caritas: Do not be fresh with me you harlot. *(walking off)*

Christina: Ha Ha. Have some fun why don't you. Please don't lose a sense of humour sister, or this misery will kill you. She is not all she purports to be. Please be careful, maybe reconsider. It is not too late.

Myrtle: My mind is made up (*starting to cry*) I am decided on the path.

Christina: She has an undue influence on you.

Myrtle: No she doesn't, don't be silly. This is my decision totally. I am my own person, just like you are. We just chose different paths. I am not made like you Christina. You are Papa's girl. You have his spirit and zest for life.

Christina: I shall miss you. You have to be sure you are doing the right thing. Please search your heart to be sure.

Act 1 Scene 3 - Living with a large family in Wijkc, the poor man's district in Utrecht. Resistance involvement. Free from Nazis but not free from denouncers. 1941

Christina: Anthonius, where have you been?

Anthonius: (*arriving home and closing the door behind him and another man*) Gerrit is here. We need to talk.

Christina: Hello Gerrit, would you like a beer you two?

Gerrit: Hello there. Yes please.

Anthonius: Yes please my darling.

Christina: Here you are. I'll leave you to it. I have to get the next batch of bread ready.

Gerrit: When do you stop Christina?

Christina: No one else can do it.

Anthonius: This is nothing to what she used to do is it dear? When she ran her father's bakery, in Lijnmarkt, a kind of Jamin shop, it was even more hard work.

Christina: None of my lazy sisters would help. They left it to me and just lived off the profits. I had the license though, so I was not working hard for nothing.

Anthonius: She certainly gave the people from the NSB down the road a run for their money. They always thought themselves better than anyone else.

Christina: They did certainly. But I was having none of it. I used to tell them to get to the back of the queue where they belonged as they were invariably the last to appear. I don't know who they thought they were. I would do it again in an instant.

Anthonius: You are fearless my sweet.

Gerrit: I suppose they have known you for years so they see nothing different in your behaviour.

Christina: It is not a political act, just a human response to the breaking down of orderly society. I will not stand for it. They don't like it. My sister and her crony friend Caritas are always telling me off for, as they see endangering our families. They are fence sitters the pair of them, like so many religious people.

Gerrit: There is no time for such people. Resistors or Collaborators are the only people that one can trust.

Christina: Collaborators, really?

Gerrit: Of course you know where you stand with them. It's the silent ones that cause the trouble because no one knows what to do with them. They could be neutral, but I hardly think that is the case, if in being neutral they watch their fellow citizens marched off to the cattle trucks or shot for assisting Jews or other so called asocials.

Christina: Yes, I can see that now.

Anthonius: I wonder if you can actually do both, partly to save your own skin but also to beat the occupiers at their own game.

Christina: I suppose that is a fine line though. I choose not to make it about politics or whether I agree with them or their dogma but instead it is about human decency and no one jumps the queue in my shop. That is the crux of how I operate in life.

Gerrit: I hope the NSB bastards and the Nazis accept that.

Christina: They do seem scared of me.

Gerrit: That may not always be the case. Be careful!

Christina: I shall.

Anthonius: Someone needs to tell you. We have to be careful always now. We cannot afford to upset these people.

Christina: Are you Dutch, husband?

Anthonius: You know I am.

Christina: You grew up near the German border. Ha Ha! Perhaps a mongrel got over the fence.

Gerrit: She has you there my friend.

Anthonius: Whose side are you on?

Christina: That is an interesting phrase you choose to use. *(Smiles at him ruefully and he looks back at her quizzically then looks away)*

Gerrit: Their arrogance is going to be their downfall.

Anthonius: Whose?

Gerrit: The Nazis of course.

Anthonius: But we mustn't let ours be ours.

Christina: What riddles you spin husband.

Anthonius: No riddles just a plain warning. If we want to beat these bastards we have to be clever.

Christina: And that is you is it?

Gerrit: Now now children! Remember we are on the same side. We cannot afford the luxury of fighting each other; we need all our energy to fight the true enemy here. Come on kiss and make up. (*Anthonius and Christina hug each other and laugh a little*)

Christina: I still have to be true to myself darling.

Anthonius: And so do I, especially when it comes to protecting my family.

Christina: I know. These are hard and complex times and we all must shift as we see fit. *(leaves the room)*

Gerrit: Well said there. None of us can truly judge another for the ways in which we get through this horror. Anthonius: (*whispers*) Maybe you can be a Collaborator *and* a Resistor. But I think many would not understand that.

Act 2 Scene 1 - Antonius has a garage elsewhere and is visited by a Nazi to organise deliveries of produce in his van. The Nazi has had this idea after seeing the van around the place. 1941
(Anthonius is in his garage, and there is a knock on the door, which when he does not immediately respond becomes a banging. He wipes his hands of grease and goes to the door.)

Anthonius: Hello, who is there? *(a flashlight is shone in his face making him stumble back)*

Nazi: Leave us. You stay here. I'll call you if I need you. *(the Nazi steps into the garage and closes the door behind him).*

Anthonius: *(gulping)* How can I help you Sir?

Nazi: Well I am not sure exactly. Let me see! You have a tidy operation here. I wonder if you might be able to work for me. We could offer to enlarge your premises in order to facilitate the work better. Maybe a pit for easier repairs of vehicles, I can arrange for that to be made by some of the Jewish scum that we have available.

Anthonius: What sort of repairs are you looking for Sir?

Nazi: Quiet let me finish. You run a delivery service, I think.

Anthonius: Yes Sir I do. We cover quite a large radius.

Nazi: And you know the border country well I know. I make it my business to know my colleagues well. You will find this if you ever try to cross me.

Anthonius: I will do what I can Sir.

Nazi: Let me say this. We need many things sorting out, including thwarting the blossoming Resistance movement and its tactics to slow us down. The other night, they laid sharp metal objects in the road in a bid to ruin the tyres of our vehicles. We will need you sometimes to clear such obstructions away. Can you do that?

Anthonius: Yes Sir we can do that for you. When can I expect the pit to be made Sir? Who will make it?

Nazi: We will arrange a work party and the work itself can begin at the end of this week. I will be in touch tomorrow with details. I will send a subordinate. I do not expect to have to come down into this district again. Do you understand me.

Anthonius: I understand Sir. Leave it to me.

Nazi: Alright. *(leaving)* Remember I am relying on your full cooperation.

Anthonius: Yes Sir. *(Nazi leaves and Anthonius busies himself after locking the door)*. Gerrit: You can come out now.

Gerrit: This man is playing right into our hands.

Anthonius: How do you mean?

Gerrit: He is commissioning a pit to be paid for by the Nazi machine.

Anthonius: But that just helps them doesn't it?

Gerrit: No man it helps us too!

Anthonius: I don't see it.

Gerrit: You have a large garage. You will get a pit made by slave labour.

Anthonius: Yes

Gerrit: Well whilst the pit is being constructed we can build a second one alongside it.

Anthonius: What for?

Gerrit: You oaf! (*pause*) To hide Jews of course. Right under the Nazi's noses. It is a master stroke. You need to get the plans from the Nazi and we will get a group together to work on the second pit at night. They will never know.

Anthonius: Genius! I can do their bidding in some small way whilst saving those they seek to oppress and kill. It appeals to my sense of the paradoxical. There are all sorts of things I can do to make them think I am on their side and yet be sabotaging their every effort at the same time.

Gerrit: I thought you might like it.

Anthonius: Please do not tell Christina. She wouldn't agree to it.

Gerrit: Oh, I don't know! I think she may well love the idea but I shall respect your wishes.

Anthonius: She never comes here so it is safe enough.

Gerrit: I will return in a week or so to see how things are progressing. In the meantime, keep your head and do as they ask. Goodbye for now. (*exits*)

Anthonius: No not that way. Go out the back. You never know who may be watching.

Act 2 Scene 2 - Anthonius meets Resistance worker Gerrit to discuss hiding Jews 1942

Anthonius: Quickly come in. Where are the people you mentioned?

Gerrit: They are around the back.

Anthonius: Let me open the door for them. *(rushing to the back door to let people in, opening the door and beckoning them into the garage)* Please come in as quickly as you can. *(Four people enter, a man, a woman and two teenage boys, swathed in scarves and hats and big coats)*

Gerrit: This is Anthonius. He is your host. *(Anthonius steps down into the pit and opens a trap door leading to the second pit)*

Anthonius: I am sorry it is so cramped but you will be safe here under the noses of the Nazis. My mechanic knows you are here and will protect you.

Jewish Man: Thank you so much Sir. You are Righteous indeed.

Anthonius: It is the least I can do.

Gerrit: Come now we must get you settled. Please follow me. *(going into the second pit and family following)*

Jewish Woman: Thank you kind Sir.

Gerrit: Now be at peace my friends and find your places here. I will be back tomorrow evening with supplies and news of your family and friends. *(Gerrit slips out of the front door so as not arouse suspicion)*

Jewish Man: I heard that you were known for collaborating with the Nazis, or at best helping them where you could.

Anthonius: Yes I know that is what people say of me. But don't you see? It is a perfect cover for me. I never do anything to assist the Nazis directly against your people but instead work on the periphery of the Nazi war machine. It is they who paid for your shelter to be made, but of course they do not realise to what extent they are supporting you all.

Jewish Woman: I don't care what it is you do. You have saved my family and I bless you for it.

Anthonius: When I make deliveries for the Germans, I also slip in extra for those in hiding in the dunes. Times are hard for us all so we must all do what we can. Working for them means I can get to travel around unhindered. It is a risk but a low one. Where are you from?

Jewish Boy: Amsterdam. Things are bad there. We are so grateful to be away.

Anthonius: Things are easier here, by no means easy, but better, I think. Were you studying there, with your brother maybe?

Jewish Boy: Yes. We were both studying until they forbade it.

Jewish Man: They both had dazzling careers ahead of them. Medicine and the Law.

Jewish Woman: Let us hope all is not lost and that they can catch up after the all this madness is over.

Anthonius: I do hope so for all our sakes. Do you have enough here to be able to rest this night?

Jewish Woman: Yes, we do; of course, thank you. We will not give you cause to regret your decision to help us. We will be quiet and cooperative.

Anthonius: I am sorry you even have to be here, in this environment and with no guaranteed end in sight. *(a bang on the door)* Hurry get inside. *(the family get into their hiding place and Anthonius closes the concealed entrance).*

Nazi: Open up. Quickly. *(Anthonius checks the place to make sure there is nothing incriminating left about and then goes to the door and opens it)* There you are. I expect you did not think you would see me again.

Anthonius: What can I do for you Sir.

Nazi: Well I am in need of your assistance right now.

Anthonius: Really Sir. What is it? *(getting his coat because sensing there is a need for him to leave with the Nazi).*

Nazi: Some local scum have strewn the road with sharp metal objects in order to blight our at- tempts to get around the area. We need these clearing away and fast. We need you to do this now. You can get rid of these objects too. I do not want to see them again. You'll go now. Quickly.

Anthonius: Yes Sir. Where are they located?

Nazi: Check with my man outside, he has the details and will drive you there. Go now*! (Anthonius leaves, but Nazi Man stays and looks around, Christina arrives from the back door and is shocked to find the Nazi Man there. She is unaware of her husband's hiding of the Jews so is open and honest with the Nazi Man).*

Christina: Hello Sir, can I help you?

Nazi: Who might you be?

Christina: I am wife to the owner.

Nazi: I am sorry; I was not aware he was married. He has gone off to do some work for me. I was just taking a look around.

Christina: Please help yourself Sir.

Nazi Man: Oh no matter my dear. I have seen enough. A pleasure to meet you.

Christina: Goodbye Sir. I am happy to be of service. *(frightened but looking towards the pit she suddenly smiles)*

Act 3 Scene 1 - Christina in bakery telling off NSB person (1943)

Christina: Good morning Frau……..

Customer: Good morning. I must say that things seemed to have improved no end since the Germans arrived here. They are such more efficient.

Christina: In what way?

Customer: Everything runs on time. They make demands that our own authorities never did. Now we get things done much more quickly.

Customer 2: Apart from this queue.

Christina: I do apologise. *(addressing Customer 1)* I am sorry but there are others waiting.

Femcke: *(jumping the queue)* I need five loaves.

Christina: Do you indeed. Well I suggest you move to the back of the queue. There are others here before you. To jump the queue is most unfair. I will not stand for it.

Femcke: You know who I am though.

Chritsina: Of course, you are Femcke……… What is your point? What difference does it make?

Femcke: You had better change your attitude if want to stay safe.

Christina: Listen! I have known you since you were this high *(pointing to a foot off the ground)*

Femcke: Yes and I have known you and your family also. *(other customers nudging each other)*

Christina: You have known what kind of person I am always. Just because your sister is a nun doesn't give you the right to special treatment.

Femcke: I don't deserve special treatment because of that bitch. I am with the NSB and am supporting the Nazis in their cleaning up of our country. That kind of service merits me a queue jump.

Christina: Oh no. Nothing merits you or anyone else as a queue jumper. This is what is right and you know it. Now get to the end of the queue like anyone else would.

Femcke: You ought to be careful!

Christina: I am always. Especially in issues of morality. You do not scare me, just you be careful in future. You are not, as we are both aware, infallible.

Femcke: Who do you think you are?

Christina: I sleep at night. Do you? I know what you have done in the past.

Femcke: You make me laugh.

SS Man: What is going on here?

Femcke: This bitch is making me wait.

SS Man: Were you at this point in the queue?

Femcke: No, I was back there.

SS Man: There are some things we must insist on and common decency is one of them. We queue for a reason, to avoid anarchy. Now get back there. Don't think that badge gives you privileges. *(SS man leaves)*

Femcke: *(looking shocked and returning to the end of the queue, a long queue down the road)* Yes Sir *(grimacing at Christina who looks proud)*

Christina: Next please. What can I get you?

Customer: A loaf and a cake please.

Christina: You having a party?

Customer: No just a minor celebration of a battle won *(smiling and winking)*. Well done! *(whisper)*.

Act 3 Scene 2 - Daughter has run in with Nazis 1944

Christina: Look! Do some cleaning. I cannot be expected to do everything in this family. Your father is busy with his business and I have the bakery. Come on - your brothers and sisters all are contributing. What are you doing?

Daughter: I am trying my best. I take some messages sometimes.

Christina: What messages? Who for?

Daughter: Some people at the club.

Christina: You must be careful there, you never know who you are dealing with.

Daughter: They are all from my school though. I know them all.

Christina: But I mean you can never know who people are once they are grown up. Be careful for goodness sake.

Daughter: You do panic Mama. Everyone likes me. No one Is ever cruel or bad tempered with me.

Christina: That is what worries me.

Daughter: Why? Do you want people to be?

Christina: No of course not but it doesn't seem real. People do have little squabbles and there are some horrible people about since the Nazis took over.

Daughter: They are just like witches and we all know what happens to them in fairy stories.

Christina: We are not living in a fairy story girl. This is real. Life is to be got through and often it is bad and we must be prepared to work through it. You do need to grow up child.

Daughter: I am grown up.

Christina: It is time for me to go to work. I want you to clean the house.

Daughter: Alright Mama.

Christina: Don't get into any mischief. *(exits)*

Daughter: I won't! Don't worry. *(she begins to dust the room for a few moments and then there is a knock at the door, She rushes to the door with duster in hand and opens the door)* Oh hello, can I help you? *(an SS man stands there and daughter immediately starts to dust his epaulettes, he is surprised, then affronted and looks stern)*

Nazi: What do you think you are doing?

Daughter: But you have something on your shoulder! *(dusting him down yet again)*

Nazi: I suggest you stop that.

Daughter: I am only trying to help. *(leaning in to get another go at dusting his shoulder)*

Sister: Come away stop that, she was only trying to help Sir. Stop messing about will you. How can we help you Sir? *(Daughter stands back)*

Nazi: I am looking for your father.

Sister: I believe he is out doing deliveries to the barracks Sir.

Nazi: Argh I see. Good. Please tell him to report to me when he gets back. Don't look so worried. I have another job for him.

Sister: Of course Sir. I think he will be going straight to the convent to speak with Sister Caritas, but when he comes home, I shall give him your message.

Nazi: Oh yes I know Sister Caritas. A good woman #, and loyal to the Reich.

Sister: She was a good friend to our aunt in the convent too before she died.

Nazi: Caritas you mean, surely not.

Sister: No, our aunt. She was always sickly. Sister Caritas has always been stronger out of our generation and although quite stern, has a heart of gold.

Daughter: Ha Ha!

Sister: Shush young one. Show some respect.

Nazi: The impetuosity of youth.

Sister: Please forgive her Sir.

Nazi: I shall be watching you my girl *(looking at daughter)* I'll let it go this time. Please tell your father to come and find me. Good day to you. *(walking away and Sister closing the door).*

Sister: Why did you do that? Are you mad?

Daughter: It's alright.

Sister: They are not so gullible as you think. Of course, they have no sense of humour but they can be so easily outraged in their arrogance. You must be more careful. Your Mama is the same, pushing it all the time with the queues in her shop. She ought to be more careful.

Daughter: Don't talk about Mama like that. She has integrity and is brave.

Sister: Or stupid. *(daughter slaps Sister)* OW! You bitch. You deserve all you get you stupid girl. They will come for you when you finally push things too far.

Daughter: They will have to catch me first?

Sister: Catch doing what?

Daughter: Nothing.

Sister: Pulling her hair.

Daughter: Why did you do that?

Sister: Tell me what is going on?

Daughter: Sometimes I take messages from one place to another.

Sister: What kind of messages?

Daughter: I don't know, I never read them.

Sister: Are they in code?

Daughter: I told you I don't know.

Sister: But you ought to know what it is you are taking and to whom. Are you mad? They would shoot you if they catch you.

Daughter: They wouldn't do that; they just get a bit cross with things, that is all.

Sister: Grow up! These people are killers. Who gives you these messages to take? What do they tell you which convinces you to do this for them?

Daughter: They say that I have always been a good girl and that I am helping all my friends by doing it.

Sister: You need to ask more questions than that. You need to understand what is being asked of you and why.

Daughter: Why?

Sister: My point exactly. People will take advantage of you if you don't ask why. You have to know what the risks are in everything you do. You can rely on no one these days. You must not put your trust in anyone. You cannot simply hope for the best.

Daughter: What about Mama? Though she is not young anymore and she takes all sorts of risks then by your account.

Sister: She is different.

Daughter: How so?

Sister: She is cunning like grandpa. He was a real water rat.

Daughter: Ugh! A water rat, what do you mean that sound horrible.

Sister: No, its a good thing, he and now she are both clever and adaptable in any situation.

Daughter: Rats are disgusting though.

Sister: No they are not, they have a function like all other creatures. We may not like them but their reputation is much maligned.

Daughter: Well I cannot think of Mama as a rat, I just cannot. *(Daughter starts to leave and Sister goes about her work and then stops)*

Sister: Anyway, our sister, your aunt, was best off in the convent with Caritas.

Daughter: Why is that? Mama still gets upset that she took the veil.

Sister: We all are sad about it but in retrospect it was a very good thing at least one of us was protected from the Nazis. Although having said, that Caritas is a cold fish, a harsh woman, much suited to the convent life where she can Lord it over everyone. She has always been a bitch. Unchristian, if you ask me but maybe you have to be to join such an institution at her level. She is ambitious.

Daughter: Aunty was such a sweet person from my memory though, someone willing to accept what life throws at her and to take orders about her life.

Sister: Caritas dragged her into the convent with her as a kind of slave, an acolyte, someone to do her bidding. She just sat in the convent and kept her head down and appeased the bastards who are running the country. Aunty died because she was never meant for the hard life of the convent. Caritas is tough and will survive us all for decades to come. She has the power and she knows how to use it to her advantage. She won't be struggling during the occupation that is for sure. Those kinds of people never wrestle with problems. When it's over, she had better watch out though.

Daughter: You don't like her, do you?

Sister: Oh go on about your business. Time for talking is over. Don't go repeating anything I have said alright?

Daughter: No, I won't.

Sister: I mean it. Or the Water Rats will get you.

Daughter: Ugh! (she leaves)

Act 3 Scene 3 - Set in a social care home housed in a former convent. Date is 5am on the 10th October 1989

(A small, barren room with an unkempt old lady, Christina, lying in her bed with an empty wheelchair, by her side, she is unable to use her right hand following a stroke. The room is spotless and sparsely furnished, no carpets, just whitewashed walls, a single dark wardrobe and a small table with an ewer and bowl set. There is ice on the windows. Nothing personal can be seen in this room except a small wedding photograph from the 1920s. The bride and groom look carefree and happy, the groom slightly stiff in his starched collar and the bride timid and nervous looking, in her dress, but still strong personally. The bride is the old woman in bed. The overriding feeling of the room is that of a solitary cell and in fact this room used to be a cell, not a prison one as one might assume but a nun's one from a time when this Dutch convent was bursting at the seams with new novices and postulants, unlike now. A four-foot-high crucifix dominates the room, it is shiny and black and some might say homoerotic and fetishistic as a result. The hanging Christ is behind the old lady looking down on her with his benevolent and beatific smile, belying his suffering. She is apparently oblivious, blank faced and bent over herself on her side in bed. A bell rings, a proper bell, not an electronic one, this signals the awakening of the whole building, although the disgruntled nuns have been at their devotions since 4am. The old lady knows that Sister Caritas will be along very soon, this is a mixed blessing as Christina knows only too well. She starts to try to sit upright as Sister does not like to have to tussle with her if she can help it. It is very hard with half of her body dead though; she can roll from her left side but has no brakes once she is upright and often rolls over right across to her right side.
Sister Caritas enters the room. She does not look at Christina and says nothing. She immediately falls to her knees before the Christ and genuflects wildly. She begins to pray……. Sister Caritas is a tall, gaunt woman, who is only

a little less aged than her charge, she is rigid in her physicality and her manner.

LIGHTS UP (Sister Caritas enters from Stage Left).

Sister Caritas: Prayer to the Lord Jesus Christ, Crucified (soft voice) O Lord Jesus Christ, Son of the Living God, Creator of heaven and earth, Saviour of the world! Behold I, unworthy and most sinful of all, having humbly bent the knees of my heart before the glory of Thy majesty, sing of Thy Cross and sufferings, and I offer thanks to Thee, the King of All and God, for that Thou hast willingly borne all the labours and troubles, temptations and agony as a man, that Thou mightiest be a compassionate Helper and Saviour to us all in every sorrow, need and dis- tress. I know, O Almighty Master, that all these things were not needful unto Thee, but rather that Thou didst bear the Cross and suffering for the salvation of mankind, that Thou mightest redeem us all from the enemy's bitter servitude. And what shall I give Thee in return, O Lover of Mankind, for all that Thou hast suffered for the sake of me, a sinner? I know not, for my soul and body and all my goods are Thine, as I too am Thine. Hoping only on Thy loving kindness which is beyond reckoning, O Merciful Lord, I sing Thine ineffable patience, I praise Thy condescension which is beyond words, I glorify Thy boundless mercy, I adore Thy most pure Passion, and in love I venerate Thy wounds, and cry out: Have mercy on me a sinner, and make Thy Holy Cross to be not without fruit in me, so that, partaking here of Thy sufferings, I may be granted to see also the glory of Thy Kingdom in heaven! Amen. *(She stands, smoothes down her robe and still without speaking roughly pulls at Christina's left shoulder and drags her out of the bed so she is sitting on the side of the bed, huffing and puffing and clearly in pain already, but not connecting with Christina at all otherwise).* You're a dead weight, a liability, like you always were. It's a long way now from that dance hall when you met that brute of a husband of yours. You cannot dance around now making a show of yourself. All these other women in here are easy because they cooperate, but not you, bitch! *(Loud voice)* This is what you do to me. *(stretching and clutching at her side).* Shift yourself in the presence of our Lord! Come on it's not that difficult. If the spirit is in you, he'll make sure you can do what is necessary. I don't know how you have the gall to get yourself brought in here. When have you ever had a Christian thought or action, living down at that rough end of the city? No self-respecting person would stay there when they could improve themselves. It shows what kind of woman you have always been. No good. At least your dear sweet departed sister found peace and security alongside me here in the convent.

(Christina sits deathly still the room is freezing and she is only wearing a soiled cotton night dress) Come on make an effort you lazy good for nothing woman! *(Sister roughly tugs at her nightie and holding her side as the pain increases, not caring about the obvious pain that Christina is in as she does so, Christina has clearly soiled her nightdress and this is now sticking to Christina as Sister Caritas starts to push her around).*

You have no answer for that you dumb wench do you? There are many others who have more right to be here than you. You must have tricked someone or bought them off.

(looking behind to Christina who has soiled the bed again) You shit and piss at will and expect me to mop up after you. Fucking whore! May God forgive me for that. It's true though - what a fucking mess you made of your life. No self-discipline. Jesus Christ! Your sister had the right idea. She listened to me and I took her under my wing. She knew what was good for her and her life and when the Nazis came, she was protected at least for a while. *(Sister Caritas genuflected and then pulls Christina's hair so forcefully that her head is pulled right back)* You bring out the worst in me.

It's your fault that those blasphemous words leave my lips. *(tugging on her hair again).* Look at the state of you! It's a good job we have these rubber sheets, you truly are a daughter of the Wijkc, they know no better the inhabitants of that shit hole. *(She pulls at the sheet almost dislodging Christina from the bed. Sneering and walking to the table she pours cold water into the bowl from the cracked ewer, grabs an old grey threadbare flannel and coming back, pushes behind Christina to clean the rubber sheet)* That nappy is supposed to mop up most of your mess, but you dirty bitch. you have still managed to overflow it. Where does all this shit come from anyway? You hardly eat anything. You seem to grow it. *(pinching Christina's skinny arm)* Nothing to say for yourself I suppose, even if you could raise that matted head up to look at me. *(pulling at Christina's head)* You're fucking useless now aren't you? Can't move, *(tugging at her bad arm)*, can't speak *(pushing her head back and opening her mouth and twisting it)* can't think either. Just a pointless lump of flesh, *(prodding her in various places and then pushing her back down onto the bed, Christina wincing as she lands on a wet rubber sheet and her own mess on her nightdress, shocked by the wet and the cold).* For fuck's sake! *(Sister crosses herself as Christina landing in the bed rubs her soiled nightdress on Sister's habit, she slaps Christina's face)* The dough you used to knead at your bakery had more life in it than you have now. At least it would rise *(looking at the Christ figure)* like our Lord did, but look at you. No one is coming to see you, so you don't need cleaning up. You'll do as you are. *(Sister Caritas pulls Christina back up to a sitting position where Christina sits on the edge of the bed still soiled and disheveled, her head bowed down. The nun takes a simple dress from the wardrobe and harshly pulls up each of Christina's arms and feeds them through the arm holes and tugs down the dress over her torso, the stain on Christina's tummy immediately bleeds through the thin cotton of her dress. The nun takes a hairbrush and roughly makes a parting and after a few strokes puts the brush down again,*

*and once again Christina is pushed down on the bed and
has her dress pulled down, streaking it with yet more mess.
She is then lifted violently and dumped in the wheelchair)*
Now I have others to see to. Its a wonder I can see to them
after seeing to you. You make me heave with your messing
about. You'll be the death of me you useless piece of shit.
(Exit Sister SL with stained sheets, flannel and bowl.)

Christina: *(suddenly straightening up, stretching and
standing up, agitated and watching and fearful, afraid of the
return of Caritas throughout her monologue)* Praise be the
witch has gone. You know all that was for show. I have
more spirituality and humanity in my little finger. I don't have
a problem with the words but you can tell when someone
spouting them is bullshitting. A lot of so called righteous,
pious, God-fearing priests and nuns have just learned the
liturgy by heart, that's all. Allow me to present myself to
you. Apparently I may not be able control my bowels,
(clutching at her night gown) to walk, to hold myself up, to
use my right arm, to speak or show due respect to him
(looking up at Jesus statue) but let me tell you I can still
think *(beginning to skip around the cell)*. There is a voice
and movement still inside me and *(looking at the audience)*
with your help I can reveal that to you now *(dancing a little)*.
Nothing that old bitch can do will change this fact of my
inner person still lives on. It's fun to play with her, to be the
helpless supplicant sinner to let her voice her hatred and
bigotry. She thinks that I have a nerve getting myself
installed in here as you heard. She calls me a daughter of
Wijkc but I am not, I am from the countryside. My husband
and I only came to Wijkc when work drew him there. We
had no idea just how rough it was, how could we? We
should have known though as the police headquarters were
right on the boundary of the area and later on the Nazis
would never go there. *(standing still and looking vacant)*
Folks lived honestly there though within the constraints of
extreme poverty. Everyone made their own way and the
authorities let the area rot so what did people expect?

(Christina hears Caritas coming and sits back down adopting her vacant persona)

Sister Caritas: *(comes back in)* You must think I have nothing better to do you dirty tart. *(genuflecting in the direction of the Christ figure).* You ought to be working for your keep instead of just sitting there, you useless old crone. *(she starts to clean the old towel and the mop bucket).* Why you can't control yourself in the night I don't know. Shit everywhere as usual. It's a waste of my energy to keep washing your arse and your bed. You're not there anyway, just a sitting corpse, which makes it easier to punish you eh. *(making a slapping gesture)* That is not so pleasurable as it would be if you were *compis mentis* though. Oh, that'll do for you today. No one's coming to see you anyway. That stupid girl of yours always gives us warning that she is visiting. *(Exit Stage Left)*

Christina: *(awake again)* My husband Toon and I never toed the line. We both resisted the Nazis in our own ways but she insists that my husband was a collaborator pure and simple, and at other times because I too didn't hold my tongue, that made things worse for her and others. To her we're just miserable sinners and ignorant fools, she's surprised that her precious Lord even bothers with me. *(walking around now in the limited space of her cell and staring at the crucifix)* She thinks I am beaten, gone, an empty shell of my former self but I have had a great life, often hard, still a life, not locked up in this dump for decades festering with hatred or with prejudice and assumptions about people. *(Staring out blankly into the auditorium)*

(Christina hears Caritas returning and falls into a comatose state once more. Sister Caritas enters again)

Sister Caritas: *(looking strained and in pain)* That fat old hag Agnes next door is dead. There'll be no more time for seeing to the tart at the other side today until lights out. It'll be her turn soon I dare say, at least I hope so, forgive me sweet Jesus. God works in mysterious ways though and not always in a way we would like. We mustn't challenge his will even so; we get the life we deserve according to God's law. *(Continues to busy herself again and then exits Stage Left)*

Christina: *(sitting in the wheelchair again and looking back at the empty bed, facing outwards to the auditorium).* Of course, I'm sad about the situation I find myself in. It is never easy to find yourself unable to function as you once could, but my philosophy has always been, be in the moment, deal with whatever life presents to you. I am amazed that that woman still holds a grudge against me and my family though; she must be eaten up inside. It is 44 years ago since all that madness ended. You would think that there would be something more up to date for her to worry about. *(standing up again and looking downstage)* She was a new postulant back then, still stuck between two worlds, but it seems now that she is truly fixed in the religious life with all that entails just like so many women in Holy Orders. I and my sisters on the other hand took on my father's bakery after he died and I being the natural leader and the others being happy to let me do just that allowed me to get on with it (miming a leadership role). During the War we kept the official papers to run the bakery, after all the Germans, needed bread as well. They didn't get preferential treatment though not them or those people from the NSB, they all expected to jump the queue but I wasn't having that. I used to say to them "You wait your turn" *(wagging a finger)* and they did, because I meant it. It was my shop and my system and all my customers were equal in my eyes. I suppose it looked like a kind of resistance but I never thought of it like that (thoughtful). My daughter on the other hand got herself caught being a courier for the Resistance. It was lucky our friend was able to talk the Nazis around into believing she was just a stupid young girl.

It was a bad shock I can tell you but afterwards I felt proud *(standing upright)*. Do you know when they came for her, she went to the door with a duster and flicked the Gestapo man's shoulders with it? I suppose she thought she was getting some dust off him or shit *maybe (mime dusting and a look of disgust)*. I had to laugh and admire her for that no matter how insane it was, although no more than my way of speaking to the Nazis and NSB back then. She had no sense of danger or forethought but nevertheless she survived the war intact. She used to be my husband's favourite before she got married; they used to do lots of things together, but her husband was rounded up in the Razzias, and actually went to Berlin to work for the Nazis in an armaments factory. Somehow my husband thought he had betrayed the people in the Netherlands by not resisting or escaping but his mother insisted that he and his brother went to work for the Nazis so she would know where her sons were. My sister, another nun, also was critical of her. "She is a fallen woman" she said, not in the sense of selling herself but more that she had shamed the family by marrying beneath her. *(Agitated as she can hear the nun coming back, she sits back down in the wheelchair and becomes the stroke victim once more)*

Sister Carltas: *(Enters and starts to prepare a small tray of food, a gruel type mush, blended down for a stroke victim, Sister looks bored with this task already and starts to talk to herself)*. Right! You'd better not make a fuss today. What a pig you are! No control of yourself anymore. You're just an animal really *(Christina knows she's getting food but there is no care if there ever was any, it's just like feeding time down at the farm)*. No fuss today righ? I don't need you messing about today of all days. *(Holding her side again and wincing with pain)*. I've got to lay out Madame van Baerle later, she's dead as I told you, but why tell you anything I don't know. You don't know what I am saying do you. *(laying down the small tray of food and preparing to feed Christina)* Come on head up. *(tugging at Christina's* *hair and pushing in a spoonful of food into her mouth)* Why can't you help me just a little, pig. *(Letting Christina's head drop violently)* you helped plenty of those miserable Jews back in the war, so why not me now. (*Tugging at Christina's hair again and shovelling in another spoonful of food, which she regurgitates all over her dress and Sister's hand).* I suppose you were a communist back then along with the resistance rabble down in Wijkc, I can understand why the Nazis didn't go down there. *(shaking off food from her hand and splashing it into Christina's hair)* Disease was rife, filthy people and their disgusting habits, there was crime too, perfect for the Red bastards to attract members. Now come on I haven't got all day! *(speeding up the feeding, Christina chokes again and lots of food this time)* Fucking dirty sow *(crossing herself in penitence and stopping for a moment to get a grip of her anger and sorting out the food on the spoon again)* At last the Communists have fallen though *(sitting beside Christina and feeding her the gruel, not caring whether it spills on her dress or not).* That damn wall is down at last. No more fuss. As of yesterday no more Cold War. I hated the bother of it all, Commies and Nazis - what a load of monsters. I can expect an easy life from now on, if you and the other bitches here behave yourselves. Those damn Nazis made such a mess, and you and your husband didn't help trading with them as you did *(shovelling another spoonful of food into Christina's mouth, making her choke and regurgitate).* What was he thinking? As for that stupid daughter of yours, still gullible even now judging by stupid remarks at the meeting with the Mother Superior last week. You people have no gratitude, no sense of what we do for this community. *(giving another spoonful, using the spoon to clean the mess from her dress, digging it into her chest).* We all needed to just accept things as they were back then and hope for the Germans to treat us well. At least the church knows where its duties lie. We have never let anyone down. You mere mortals have no sense of the truth. *(one last spoonful of gruel given to Christina in a derisory way, the Sister gets up and winces with pain once more whilst bending double, and places the bowl on the table and starts to go, turns around and stares at Christina)* You'll be the death of me unless God gets you first. That would do us all a favour wouldn't it. *(Pain again doubles Sister Caritas up)* Not so mouthy now are you, *(gritting her teeth against the pain)* silent as the grave, which is good preparation for where you're going. No need for a voice in the inescapable flames of Hell. You were always wanting to bring attention to yourself you were, making things bad for all of us with your rudeness and that husband of yours sucking up to those people as well. Well enjoy your day, at least you have time now to reflect on what you have done and what you have come to, by God's good grace. His purpose is strong and inescapable. *(Exit Sister Caritas bearing the tray, she grabs the edge of the door frame for a few moments and regains her composure after another bout of pain and then carries on slowly out of the room).*

Christina: *(suddenly straightening up, stretching and standing up, agitated and watching and fearful, afraid of the return of Caritas throughout her monologue).* See what I mean? *(looking down at her dress).* Nuns have a lot to answer for. As for human kindness, forget it. *(Standing up again).* So my daughter was hemmed in all-round by criticism, except from me though, I didn't criticise her choice. I just worried about what it would mean for her. So you see, we all have our opinions and these can be so hurtful. I for one was very sad when my sister made the choice to join this convent life. *(looking around her cell and sitting down for a moment and gathering herself still upright and apparently perfectly well, she is perplexed by the state of herself, soiled clothes and rough hair, she attempts to tidy herself up).* That's better. I have to be ready in case the scraggy old shit comes back and there is no point standing when you don't have to. *(Brushing her hair back and falling backwards into the seat a little more and closing her eyes and then opening them again)* Years at the bakery taught me that valuable lesson. Do you know my daughter didn't even realise how long a pregnancy is? I suppose I should have talked to her more, but we were brought up to just get on with it, it's a natural process after all, rather like death. I've seen a lot of that and there is no avoiding it when it comes. My husband was quite a prude though and frowned upon that kind of talk. He was strict and just expected things to be just so and he had a rigid view of a woman's place being in the home and not in society. *(smiling inwardly)* I sometimes used to sneak off with my brother on a delivery for my husband and in the country my brother would let me drive. Back then cars did what they were told, you just steered them in a certain way and they went that way. It wasn't complicated like now. I relished these trips. I felt free in a way. I suppose like Toon on the water. If my husband had known he would have beaten me. *(looking wistful)* He was not liked particularly, but he and I got along somehow, it's all give and take isn't it? When we first met, he loved me so much, he'd take me sailing, I was his Fokkejongen, a kind of helper to change the sails and so on. It was amazing because to this day, I cannot swim, but Toon was a Water Rat in so many ways, which was useful for the whole family. He was able to manoeuvre himself on land and sea and balance things in his life to always give us the support we needed. He had been a custom man at Lobith, checking German ships for opium, which they would confiscate, he and his friends used to smoke it for themselves too but then afterwards he found respectability in a bicycle shop in Vreewijk, where I was from.

(Sound of footsteps along the corridor, Christina falls back into her wheelchair and her former physicality, head bowed and right arm hooked like the claw of a bird, the lost human is back)

Sister Caritas*: (Sister Caritas enters stage left with accoutrements of laying out, cotton sheets, basin and sponge etc)* These old bags never get any easier, especially when they are dead. She is 146 kilos, that damn van Baerle woman. *(Stretching her back out, hands on her painful body)* They send us in alone to do the washing now, and this is supposed to be progress. It was never like this in the convent days. We would have three or even four of us to wash the bodies. Now all I can do is push them over on their sides and life one leg at a time to clean their private parts. She was a good woman in the war though, Madame van Baerle, she kept her mouth shut until it was all over and never complained whilst she was in here, God rest her. She was a model citizen, kept her head down and didn't cause problems. Unlike you. I'd better go and get her dressed now before the undertaker comes. *(Exits stage left)*

Christina: *(Suddenly straightening up, stretching and standing up, agitated and watching and fearful, afraid of the return of Caritas throughout her monologue).* I am glad she has gone again; I never know what she gets up to next door but I can hear when she has gone out. It's too dangerous to venture in there though. *(Facing at auditorium centre stage onstage right)* You know, it's just so tedious to face that deluge of abuse from her. I've had much worse over the years though. She was going on and on about the end of the Cold War as though It was set up to annoy her personally, the same way she feels my family's mission was to destroy her easy life. What do I know about that damn wall anyway? It's obviously a black and white issue for her. The wall comes down, the Communists stop making trouble like when the Nazis were hounded out of the Netherlands in 1945, and she will be able to go back to her serene life, *(walking serenely with hands in praying motion)* way up on the moral high ground above war and life and dirt, apart from me and the others here of course who are a timely and comical reminder of just how messy life can get *(looking at her bed and then her dress and suddenly becoming serious as she remembers something important).* Talking of mess and one created by her and her sisters. *(looking sad)* I remained quiet about this to protect my children some years ago and chose to do that over attempting to right a wrong done against many children in the Netherlands at that time. I live with that decision every day as one must often live with such things but I stopped one wicked person which I feel was a good thing. I made sure she could never have access to her chosen victims again. That woman, Sister Caritas, I hesitate to call her that, is a sexual and physical abuser of children, one of many in the church. *(getting angry)* Now as you can see, she vents her outrage on us, her charges, because we are vulnerable which gives her a heightened sense of her own power and she assumes we cannot answer back or report her *(a look of superiority comes to her face).* Yet she knows what I know and has some shame still which impels her to grudgingly see to my needs as she calls it. *(pulling her dress out to how she actually cares)* She owes her position to me as I agreed to drop the charges brought against her and to enable her to continue to be a nun. This may seem harsh to you, unforgivable even, *(a pause and she hangs her head down)* but the Church was and remains massively powerful and back then no one would touch the defending of such a case. The only thing that would have happened would have been hell for all our children. and being vilified by our community. There was not one lawyer I could find who would take on the church at that time. Life is never really as black and white *(looking resigned)* as we would have it be, despite what Caritas says. *(sitting down once more suddenly very tired and looking lovingly at her bed with no sheets, she hangs her head down she drifts back into her real self, head bowed and her bird like claw coming back, she remains silent for some time and then drifts off to sleep.)*

Sister Caritas: *(Sister Caritas enters Stage Left again looking very very red faced and exhausted)* Good grief I am not as young as I was. I'll be in one of these places myself soon at this rate. You old hags drive me mad. I signed up for a quiet and easy life, not this day in day out struggle. I saw, in my youth, just how cruel life was for a poor working-class girl, and the only option for gentrification and safety from men and the spectre of constant childbirth was the religious life. It was a sacrifice I was willing to make. All I had to do was pretend to be pious and holier than thou, and I could do get away with anything I wanted. It became my right to Lord it over everyone to compensate me for the life I had been forced to endure since becoming a nun, a life much worse than the gutters and bars of De Wallen or so it feels. Being the eldest child of 14 of our worn-out mother and our brutal sex-crazed father, it was only a matter of time before I would have been pressured into giving myself in return for his drinks money or even worse being forced to give myself to him. Thankfully I was able to avoid that hideous fate which was borne instead by my younger sisters and even a brother or two. This taught me to play the system. Having said that, in the end the system has played me in return only in a different way. *(Looking at the crucifix on the wall)* You have a lot to answer for. Bride of Christ indeed! More like a lackey and slave girl. No wonder I have sought my pleasure elsewhere. This *(looking at her habit and then at the statue of Christ)* gives me a power over other human beings that I could never have attained out in the world. How I have treated them over the years is the price I exacted for your hood-winking me all those years ago. I even got away with it and but for this bitch here I would be totally reassured as to the peace I deserve in my latter years. You actually have no power, do you? The power is with the church, with the men and to a lesser extent, we women of the cloth. I just need to see off you here once and for all. *(looking at the time on the clock with the loud ticking, Sister realises she needs to be somewhere yet again ministering to another of those women in the care home so she exits limping and holding her side)*

Christina: *(She wakes up once more, comes back to her more animated self, she sits upright, suddenly straightening*

*up, stretching and standing up, agitated and watching and
fearful, afraid of the return of Caritas throughout her
monologue).* She could make our lives better if she chose
to. She had better watch out for God's will though, because
when I die, a legal fury will be unleashed on dear old Sister
Caritas and she will be ruined and will face a 'living hell' for
what time remains to her. She thinks she has power over
me but all of this that you see today, is worth enduring to
fool her into believing that she has gotten away with it.
(*Standing up*)

It is never clear cut to say that a collaborator was wrong or
that a Resistor was too, the issues are much more complex
than that and no one knows what they would do when they
have not lived through it *(Suddenly sad).* With the Nazis
and Communists, they were monsters but I was younger
then and death an unlikely prospect, so it was easy to be
bold. With the Church issue, I was somewhat older and
more fearful and uncertain. I was a parent and that does
change things, one's attitudes I mean. It is good though to
be adaptable to change with the times and with our own
experience of life. (suddenly bold again) And now I have
been able to raise a voice for the many who have faced a
terrifying life. She still has the effrontery to judge my
husband for trading with the Nazis and NSB. The fact that
he occasionally cleaned the road when the Resistance had
spread nails to make holes in the tyres of the Nazi's cars
stuck in her craw but she never knew that he did this at
gunpoint at great risk to himself from all sides. She also
does not know to this day that my husband hid Jews in his
garage and not just one or two but many, over a long period
of time. He thought I didn't know about it, but of course I
did. Back then you didn't say much to anyone unless they
were in imminent danger. His view was that by trading with
the Nazis he could support Jewish Dutch people to evade
capture and the almost certain death they would face. By
being close to the Nazis he was able to operate a safe
house right under their noses *(erratic breathing now, she*

stops for a moment or two and then recovering herself) He was truly a water rat, comfortable on land or sea and also in any situation life threw at him. He was supremely adaptable. *(slumps again as she hears Caritas coming back)*

Sister Caritas: *(enters again)* Will they never let me have a moments peace, these cows? *(looking exhausted and visibly in pain)*. Don't you dare make life difficult for me, not now. I have a retirement coming up, my just reward for service. This bitch here is nothing but a trouble maker. *(bending double in pain)*. You bastard, after all I've done for you, *(struggling to find respite from the agony she feels)*. At least she'll never get revenge on me if you are thinking of taking me now *(looking at Christ figure)*. I know you're faking the passivity, oh I know you're a vegetable, but there must be somewhere inside you that still holds that hate she had for me and the fact that you could do nothing about the abuse you discovered. I beat you at that. Who do you think you are to accuse me? Even if it was true, you have no right to set yourself above me. You know nothing of my life, the hardships I had to endure before and after I took my vows, *(shaking her fist at Jesus)* Vows! That's a joke. Its just a set of shackles in the end, not the mystical marriage as promised. *(another burst of excruciating pain which takes Sister to her knees and then to roll around in agony on the floor)* I have beaten you because you'll be dead soon and in any case you cannot talk anymore or function at all. *(Gasping for breath between the pains)*. My memory will remain unblemished in the minds of my flock and the townspeople. *(She screams an unholy death rattle and is dead on the cell floor in front of Christina)*. You Bast…………….. *(looking at Christ and slumping on the floor dead)*

Christina: *(Knowing the look of a woman dying, looking ecstatic but also a little disappointed that she had been taken before her, which would mean she would not have to* *face the charges that would become public at her death.)* Damn! *(She goes to the door and looks outside and crosses herself and raises a fist in Sister's direction, and moves back centre stage right)* She has beaten posterity but perhaps now her victims will find some comfort and resolution, knowing she is no more. I wondered how long it would be before that venom turned in on itself. I feel that when I am facing death it will no longer matter what I went through but what I will say will still be important. That unrepentant bitch cannot harm me anymore, and I remain who I am as I have always tried to be and by making the very best choices in situations that I could. I weighed up the options in the past and on each occasion chose the course of action which I felt was best for the most. I will not be judged by her and her kind. They have more to be ashamed of than I and my family. The truth must come out if only for a small audience and it will even if she will never know how much she will be vilified as the evil abuser she is. *(resting on the bed for a moment)* I feel tired now. Where was I before she came in last time? *(looking surprised)* Wait a minute! You know it just doesn't matter anymore. I can be wherever I am now, I can rest and let Sister Immanuel care for me from now on. She is a good woman unlike that scheming bitch Caritas. Nothing matters now. I will go on until I don't, but will be happy to the end now. *(getting up and walking round and around the stage and laughing to herself)*